Twisted

A Dark Anthology

USA Today
Bestselling Author

UVI POZNANSKY

Twisted©2013 Uvi Poznansky

Published by Uviart
P.O. Box 3233 Santa Monica CA 90408
Blog: uviart.blogspot.com
Email: uvi.author@gmail.com

First Edition 2013
Printed in the United States of America
Book design, cover design, and cover image by
Uvi Poznansky

Contents

I Am What I Am

Job's Wife: a Journey through Hell

L ying still in a corner of the cave, I try my best not to rattle, not to betray my fear. I figure, as long as they think me unconscious, I am safe. I have jolted awake because of the voices, only to discover they are incoherent and muffled. In between the gusts of wind, I can hear them hissing. Each phrase plays out in some verbose foreign music, which I cannot decipher for the life of me. Sigh. This is not Aramaic for sure, or any of the other languages spoken by the locals in my village or by the merchants traveling through along the Jordan river.

At this moment I find myself overwhelmed, turned inside out by a sense of suspicion. Something has been taken away from me. My breath? My name? Identity? Who am I, then?

After an eternity, the confusion in my head starts clearing up. The air is steaming hot. It feels as if I have been dunked in some thick, dark soup. I stare at the blackness. I listen. I catch a word here and there, and somehow I get it. No longer is it Greek to me. Or perhaps it is.

"But why? What is she to you?" says a trembling, shrill voice. "Why even come here for her? Just a tramp, is what she is."

And in a grumble—louder than the whirlwind—another voice says, "Now, who are *you* to ask?"

"Forgive me... I am nothing, nothing before you. Crush me if you will. I am dust, dust under your feet... But you, you have more important things to do. Let her rot."

"Gird up now your loins like a man; for I will demand of you, and you shall answer me. Where were you when I laid the foundations of this realm? Declare, if you have any understanding!"

"I am nothing... Nothing but dust—"

"Who has laid the measures thereof, if you know? Or who has stretched the line upon it?"

"I bow," the thin voice trembles. "I bow before you. Oh please, forgive me."

And splosh! I hear the poor devil plodding away, wading through some slush.

A minute later, the footfalls of the other march up the road in the other direction, until finally the ground under me stops rumbling.

So I turn on my belly and crawl, finding my way in the dark, till at last I peek out—if only by a nose—through the mouth of the cave. Which allows me, for the first time, to take in the view.

It is breathtaking—not only because of the deep ravines slashing back and forth across the landscape, or the thick trunks of trees twining their roots one over the other, clinging forcefully to the rocky ledges; not only because of the volcanoes towering over the horizon, or the fine lava streams marbling the flesh of the earth, or that landmark, that pillar of salt beckoning me from afar, or the little flame dancing over there, then here, licking my knees—ouch!—or the bubbling of swamps along the winding path. No, it is breathtaking because to my amazement, I recognize this place.

A crimson glow is coming from below, as if an enormous sun is buried here, deep under the coals upon which I am crouching. If not for the eerie glow, this is the valley cradling my village.

A perfect copy of the land of Uz.

If I squint hard, aiming my gaze faraway to the foot of that volcano, I think I can spot the familiar outlines of houses. They belong to the rich among us. Between them I look for an interval. There must lie the village square. And I know, without really seeing it, that falling to pieces on the other side—where the poor folk live—is our shack. The place where we lived, Job and I, in such misery during the last year.

Imagining it, even for a second, frays my nerves.

And now, now the vision comes back to me, as if seeping out of the holes in this landscape, in my past. Twisted. It is accompanied by the sound of wails, which curdles my blood. In my confusion I wonder, whose voice could it be?

At first I get it wrong: I figure, perhaps it was Leila, that barefooted beggar woman, who used to come knocking at our door. I mean, when the door still hung, somehow, on it crooked hinges, and when I could still afford to toss some coins at her. I admit, it used to give me a measure of satisfaction to see her bow down before me, all the way to the ground, to pick them up. At least, there was one creature in this village who had the misfortune of being poorer than me. But not anymore. Hitting rock bottom is no fun. I hate being found empty handed. I had nothing now, nothing I could give her.

No, this was not her voice, because now I could hear the shrill yowls, the howls of anguish, punctuated with a shriek here and there, first from one throat, then another. Yes, I recall what happened. I go back to that place, back to that moment in time, hearing the fading of the singsong wails, and the unexpected burst of laughter out there in the distance.

And so I knew the mourners had started to disperse by now, which was truly humbling. Alas, they had been at it for a shorter time than usual—but how could you blame them, really?

There was no money, and of the seven thousand sheep, three thousand camels, five hundred yoke of oxen and five hundred donkeys we used to own, not a single one was left. Nothing you could offer them for payment; alas, nothing left to sustain the customary expression of grief. Sigh.

Job stayed with me awhile. Again and again he mumbled, in his inexplicable, pious manner, "Naked I came from my mother's womb, and naked shall I depart." Men! Always thinking of themselves! All the while there I was, flat on my back, in need of some attention, and some clothes, too!

Finally he left the gravesite. I waited, waited until the sound of his footfalls had shuffled away—oh, how well I knew this tortured gait of his!—until it too was gone.

All was quiet now, deadly quiet. You had to put your ear close to me to hear the one thing, the only thing that screwed up this silence: the crinkly sound of my hair and nails, continuing to grow, somehow. Even the crows had stopped echoing their calls between one and another. And yet, I was not alone. I could sense another presence.

When at last I mustered the will to blow the gravel off my eyelids and force them open, the first thing I saw was sandals. Diamond-studded sandals, no less.

Never before had I seen such an elegant design in our village—not even at my own wedding some years back, when Job could still afford spoiling me. At the time he had been considered a good catch. Rich beyond belief, and as healthy as an ox, he had not been known for being blameless or righteous until much later. Some wicked fun we had! And to please me, he would pour coins into my purse—what a delightful jingle!—so I might buy the most exotic fabrics for my dresses, and the most expensive footwear, imported by Babylonian merchants traveling through the Kingdom of Edom on their way to Egypt.

How I had been pining lately for his attention, or—failing that—for the luxury of going on a shopping spree! It would have been a pleasant distraction from all my suffering.

If only I could go, one last time, and buy some brand-new designer clothes, or better yet, shoes...

But now, these sandals—right there at my eye level—were sleek, but also quite strange. Their tar-black, impossibly high heels were cutting with a twist into the freshly dug earth; which at once, seems to scare away a host of worms.

Naturally, I tried to squirm away—but could not move a muscle.

And look: inside these two contraptions were the ugliest feet I had ever seen. Toes crooked, nails spiked, with an irregular, cracked outer edge—yet they were painted quite liberally with some blood-red smear.

Sigh. I closed my eyes. Was this a joke, or a bad dream? With such a sloppy manicure, this bitch—whoever she was—must have been even more impatient than I ever was.

I wished that—for a spell—I could take a peek, just long enough to compare our feet. Mine, you see, are so much prettier! And what's more, they had been cleaned the night before by the village women, washed once with water from the local well, and a second time with tears.

But now, even without casting a look I could tell, by the chill on my skin, that under this shroud my feet were utterly bare. No boots, no shoes, no sandals.

Which made me envy her.

Through the skin of my closed eyelids I could sense a sudden change. Blocking the sun, her shadow came crawling upon me, until suddenly it stopped. Which was when—with no warning, and no respect for the departed, either—she gripped my arm, rolled me aside and to my surprise, hopped in.

Unfortunately, there was no mistaking her smell. I used to think it was the dirt caking, layer after layer, on her bare feet. Yes, that must have explained it! But somehow it reeked even worse now, perhaps because these elegant straps of leather grazed into the dirt, peeling it from her heel. Oh hell, I croaked, wishing I could turn away.

Not now, go away, Leila.

I could hear the heavy flapping of her breast and at once, the ground under me shook. It opened—by God, the ground split open under her sharp, pointy heels, and scream! My hair was flying straight up, my jaw dropped open...

Within a second, the earthen walls grew immensely higher, they were vaulting over us and there we were— there in my grave—in a free fall—

Rising, somehow, to a shaky stand I popped my eyes open. Still, all I could see in the mounting darkness is the quick flash of her teeth. She bared them in a smile.

I turned my gaze away, noting the walls around us. I had seen an elevator once, when Job had taken me to a hotel, the King David Hotel in Jerusalem. He had booked the honeymoon suite up there at the very top, knowing it would impress a simple village girl like me. But now, this here was like no elevator I had ever seen before.

How can I begin to describe it to you? Space was tight. In distress I looked up—perhaps by force of habit—to cry, to say a prayer. Stones, torn roots, autumn leaves, most of them already rotten, even tiny lizards and worms were soaring over us in a big swirl, bouncing from time to time off the walls, and then being blown up and away with a big spit, straight off the top of this thing.

After a while you could breathe again, if you were so inclined. I was not. In the shadows, if you dared brush your fingers around you, you might feel the mud slipping upward along the walls as we went on falling.

Then came various outlines, various shells and pebbles and hairy seaweed, all floating across a layer of damp air. From time to time a fish skeleton swam by, lit from inside, like the neon signs at the top of that hotel in Jerusalem. And then, puff! The skeleton hit the elevator wall and crumbled to dust.

Layer after layer rose away. Water, vapor, gas; cold, hot, toasty. All the while the floor kept accumulating hairy strands of algae, crumpled insect wings, chopped off lizard tails, split-open pebbles, coal dust...

In the mounting pressure I could see particles start to crystalize. Here and there something seemed to glitter underfoot. My companion would swoop down greedily— before I could move a finger—and snatch it. A diamond.

Sigh. I cannot stand this woman. What a bitch.

The elevator sank deeper and deeper, farther and farther into an abyss, shaking violently as it went through its paces, giving out loud creaking noises.

Then, with an abrupt thud, it came to a stop. A zigzag fissure appeared along the wall, and before it cracked open I knew: On this side, darkness. On the other—the unknown.

Snap out of it, I tell myself. Don't allow yourself to drift away into the past. But then, before I can crawl back to safety, to the depth of the cave, a deep groan rises from down below at my left side, and from the right it is echoed back.

"Hell," I blurt. "Where am I?"

To which a voice says, "You can say *that* again."

I cast a quick glance this way and that, and see—just outside the mouth of the cave—two figures standing guard. Only they are standing upside down, perfectly frozen. Icy wings hang down from their shoulders, broken. And splinters are scattered on the dirt all around them. They are so still that it seems they have been carved from pillars of salt—if not for their feet twitching up there, above me.

Clenching my jaws so they stop clattering I manage to say, "Who are you?"

The only answer I can hear is a groan from the left, somewhat muffled this time. Turning right I bend down to take a good look at the other guard. Why is he silent?

"Who," I repeat, "are you?"

His head is now barely visible; eyes and nose already submerged, he seems to struggle for air. Mud is flowing into his white mouth, and at the surface, froth starts regurgitating.

"Fallen angels are a dime a dozen around here," grumbles a throaty voice from above. Her foot kicks some more muck in his direction. "Some," she says, "have no names at all."

Startled I look up, and by her diamond-studded high heel sandals I recognize her.

"This one," I point. "What's his name?"

Leila hisses at me, "Who cares."

"Doesn't he have one?"

"Don't you?"

Which gives me pause. My name is at the tip of my tongue and yet, I cannot utter it. Sigh. Somehow it has been erased from memory.

"Unlike you," I retort, if only to hide my frustration, "I used to have one."

"And a big fuss you made over it last night," she shoots back.

"And just how—I mean, how would *you* hear about that?"

"I was there, darling. Stood so close behind you, I could practically poke you," says Leila. "Didn't you feel my presence? I couldn't help blowing my breath at your neck, just to see you shudder... Lordy Lord, Lord of the flies! You made such a goddam stir over nothing."

And before I can catch my breath to answer, on she goes, "A poor woman such as yourself should know her place, and never argue with her man, let alone with the elders in the village! Your name is not worth all that disrespect, dear. I expected that in a second, lightning would come down to strike you down. I knew, I just knew what was coming."

"Did you," I say.

"Indeed," she says, with a hard glint in her eyes. "There I was, sniffing at your back, itching, itching, itching to take hold of you already..."

I gulp, so she goes on to say, "Unfortunately, the down elevator was broken; stuck down here in the pit. So alas, I had to bide my time."

The bitch kicks at the fallen angel again—but his time, her big toe is snagged, perhaps by a rock. "Damn, damn, damn it," says Leila. "And damn you! You and your stupid name and your stupid quibbles and fights with everyone around you."

"My name," I insist, "is all I have left."

"Not anymore," she corrects me. "It has, by now, been stripped away from you. Looking at your eyes, I can tell."

"Even so! It's still mine," I say, noting a tone of stubbornness in my voice.

"Oh, dream on," she shrugs. "And not that I care, but did you have to argue with the elders over it? Have you no civility, woman? No respect for them, or for keeping the silence in the village library?"

"Who gives a damn," I say. "Who cares about those three wrinkly prunes, decking themselves with thick furs, shuffling their fancy quills between their porcelain-white fingers as if they, and no one else but them, were the instruments of God?"

To that she can find no answer, and so I press on, "All the while there I stood, right in front of their long table, trying not to fold over with the pangs of hunger, spotting the bread crumbs on the floor, and bracing myself with nothing but my pride so I don't bend down before them."

Leila passes her gaze over me top to bottom. Then with a belittling smile she says, "You had nothing on but stained tatters, dear. Not your best attire, you must admit. Making an appearance in rags like that cannot possibly make a good impression on anyone, let along on those wise guys."

"Fashion is a crucial thing, normally," I agree. "But in this case, let me ask you: who on earth gave them the idea that they are in charge of us village folk?"

And she says, "They are the keepers of history, woman. You ingrate! You should kiss their feet for putting your ancestry in writing."

"Not mine, they don't," I say vehemently. "Oh sure, men's ancestry is carefully kept. Our land, the land of Uz is named after Uz, son of Aram, son of Shem, son of Adam. But then—women? In my village they are of less value than cattle. So you tell me: is there any purpose for keeping the ancestry of cattle?"

She scratches her head, and comes up with, "None other than breeding, I suppose—"

"Exactly! Breeding, that's what women are good for, in a man's world. So their ancestry is forgotten, their names erased, their lives become mere anecdotes. In time, they become invisible holes in the fabric of the story. It's as if they never existed."

And I hope that somewhere, in her heart of hearts she feels for me when I say, "Look: when I was a little girl I ran up a hill from my house; and across the valley I spotted a pillar of salt. I couldn't resist coming closer. I stood at her feet, looked up and met the eyes, the empty eyes of Lot's Wife. And right there and then, seeing the trail of bitter tears running down her neck, I promised myself: I will never let that happen to me!"

She shrugs.

And so I forge ahead. "The elders, all they know is how to brush their long, silvery beard, twirl the tip of it between their fragile thumb and forefinger, and once in a while, draw a cryptic glyph here, and another one there. Pricks! All they do is jot down men's lives, men's stories, men's trials and victories in a scroll that no one but them can read. They have rolls and rolls of papyrus in their fancy library. Fuck them!"

"Gladly." She winks.

"Oh hell," I say. "You don't understand."

"Fuck you," says Leila. "You were doomed, dear, the moment you opened your big mouth."

"I may be doomed," I say. "But all the same I want my name to live on. Or at least, to have a chance to do so."

"A dreamer," she says. "That's what you are."

"No," I say.

She laughs in my face. "Yes," she says. "You are seeking that which you can't have."

"I am a woman on a quest."

"Same difference. You live in a twisted phantasy. Now as then."

"Which is why I went in there, just to try, to convince them to write my story, to scribble it back in place, where it belongs—if only for a single sentence—for half a phrase, even! See, I had to act fast, before they submit this scroll to the rabbinical assembly for a possible inclusion, God willing, in the holiest book of all—"

"By which you mean, the bible?"

"Yes. The bible."

She pleats her hairy eyebrows as if to focus on a thought. Wasted effort, I think. In her place, I would think of nothing else but plucking them so I look halfway decent.

"Well," she says at last, "You may be surprised! Perhaps this place feels strange to you, but you may find it incredibly cultured. Not that I expect a simpleton like you to appreciate it, but the reopening of the Hellexandria Library is planned to happen soon. I'm pretty sure the collection will include a few editions of the bible."

"What do I care," I mutter. "I can't even read."

In a flash, Leila grips my shoulder. The uneven, blood-red polish of her nails gets caught in a dim flicker of light.

"Damn you, dear," she says with an acid smile. "Wake up, wake up already! Don't you get my drift? Perhaps, once you get to know some of the poor souls around here, you may find someone among them, someone who can read aloud for you, and recite those so-called sacred pages. Perhaps he can figure out if your precious little sentence, precious little phrase made it in after all, I mean, if your name lives on."

With that, a shadow stirs loose behind her.

Within a second it expands immensely. Then it steps forth from beyond, and is now blocking the entire view.

The earth gives a mighty thud with every step he takes, which is rather peculiar for a shadow.

Immediately, she turns from me and takes a deep bow before him. All I can see against the faint light is an outline. Crowning his head is a subtle impression of something curled. Horns.

Sigh. I may be mistaken, but I think I know who this is.

He turns to me with a sly look. To my surprise, his smile—even with those sharp fangs—is quite endearing.

"Job's wife, I presume? Hallelujah! I have been expecting you for quite a long while," says Satan. His voice is sweet. He must have sung in a choir in his youth, because in some ways he sounds as pious as my husband. "Shame, shame, shame on you." He wags his finger. "You sure made me wait, didn't you..."

And without allowing time for an answer, he brings a magnifying glass to his bloodshot eye. Enlarged, his pupil is clearly horizontal and slit-shaped.

Which makes me feel quite at home with him, because so are the pupils of the goats in the herds we used to own.

Meanwhile, Satan unfolds a piece of paper and runs his finger through some names listed there. Then, with a gleam of satisfaction he marks a checkbox there, right in the middle of the crinkled page. At once, a whiff of smoke whirls in the air.

Satan blows off a few specks of charred paper, folds the thing and tucks it into his breast pocket, somewhere in his wool. Cashmere, I ask myself? Really? In this heat?

Back home, when I would count my gold coins, this was something I craved with a passion... It would keep me warm during the long winter nights...

Then, without even bothering to look at me, Satan says, "I swear, madam, you look lovely tonight."

For a moment I am grateful that my husband is among the living. Or so I think. Nowadays, influenced by the elders, he regards swearing as a mortal sin, as bad as cursing. He even plugs his ears, for no better reason than to avoid hearing it. But if you ask me, I swear: without a bit of blasphemy, language would utterly dull, and fit for nothing but endless prayer. Sigh.

Strangely, Satan does not frighten me that much anymore. And so, swaying on my hip bones, I strut out of the cave in his direction. I feel an odd urge to fondle his horns. Along the path toward him I make sure to suck in my belly, because in the company of a gentleman, even a corpse is entitled to look her best.

"No—not a corpse," he corrects me, as if he has just read my mind. "A soul! That is what you are."

"A damned one, too," says Leila, cutting in.

And he says, "Aren't we all."

And she hisses, "Especially her. She is a nobody. She belongs with the dreamers among us; the losers."

I figure she does not like me, and she does not appreciate competition. All smiles and giggles, she is batting her eyelashes at him while wiggling her heavy bust and advancing, somehow, in the mud, over her diamond-studded sandals.

Which in a flash, angers him. In spite of a visible effort to remain calm his face turns red, and he shakes his fist at her. I spot a dark feather wagging back and forth behind his neck, nearly tickling him, which is the first clue to what happens next: wings sprout from his back, and they spread out—monstrously massive—with an furious, ear-splitting flutter.

"Go," he spurts out, no longer in control of himself. "Not now! I am busy here, can't you see?"

"With her?" says the bitch, utter disbelief ringing in her voice. "Who—what is she to you?"

And he answers, mostly to himself, "First and foremost, she is a case study. An accomplice in my plans, even though she does not recognize it—not yet. When she does, I can use her. Therefore, she is a possible ally. Even one soul can tip the scales, change the balance of power and overturn things, up and down, heaven and hell."

Then he turns to me. His wings are quivering loudly over us, to the point of making the conversation difficult. He tries to shrug, in vain. "They're great for transportation," he explains. "An occasional flight is a welcome relief from—"

And she cuts in to complete his sentence for him, "From roaming throughout the earth, going back and forth on it..."

Satan turns to her, wreathing dark fume, and with a hoarse voice he cries, "Go, go back, back to where you came from!"

She croaks, then curtsies awkwardly and shrinks from him. I see her slipping meekly back into the door of the down elevator, which is right next to the mouth of the cave, where the fallen angel on the left used to be.

The fallen angel on the right is still here, swaying in the wind—but now he has given out his last groan. Sigh.

Escaping through the zigzag crack in the door is a stifled sound, the sound of her whimpers. Alas, Leila does not take rejection too well.

"Good riddance," snarls Satan.

And with curled fangs he guzzles down some air, one, two, three times, then bites his lips, perhaps to let out some blood, to control himself, his madness. It must be working: The fume has dissipated, or perhaps swallowed with the last gulp. Now his tongue is glistening red, darting across his teeth.

And by now his wings have become transparent. They are so fine you can barely see them anymore. Only by reasoning can you guess that they have folded, that they are now coming together, ready to be tucked away somewhere between his pointy shoulder blades.

I can tell this fellow is given to mood swings, although now his fury has left him. He raises his magnifying glass to his eye once more, and with great, scientific calm he moves around me, licking his lips and examining me closely, as if I were an interesting specimen.

Then he winks at me, suggestively so.

Which is quite familiar to me. Since the downfall, every man in the village has tried his hands on me, so to speak.

"Stop that," I say pluckily. "You know I am a married woman."

I notice that Satan does not mind my chutzpa. Quite the opposite: he seems to enjoy a spirited reply. Perhaps the poor souls living in his realm have no balls.

Meanwhile, a strange thing crosses my mind: the valley out there, in the distance, is vacant; eerily so. Dare I ask?

And before I know it, I can hear myself saying, "I see the fallen angels here—what remains after them—but where are the rest? I mean, where are the demons?"

Satan leers at me, and his voice resonates deeply, suddenly penetrating the depth of my soul.

"Where else?" he says. "Inside."

Then he walks down the path, not before waving his hand with an elegant, courteous gesture, which I take to mean, Come now! Come with me!

Which I do—even though with each step, my feet get more and more scalded by the boiling earth. But I don't give a damn, this pain cannot stop me, nothing can, because somehow I know there is a purpose to this journey. In life or death, I am—and perhaps always will be —a woman seeking a name for herself.

A woman on a quest.

We are traveling together in the direction of my village. Well, the copy of it. As close as can be.

Home.

And when we arrive at long last at the edge of the village I run back and forth, looking for my shack. All in vain. It has been completely erased. Wiped off the map, just like my name. Sigh. Is this a lie? An imperfect replica of my birthplace? A dream, an alternate reality, conjured for my eyes only? I wipe them over and again, utterly tortured by my doubts.

Meanwhile Satan leads me away to the village square and with a big flair, opens a door.

This is the largest building in our village, the library where I met the three elders just the other night—or was it once upon a time, ages ago? With each step I take, echoes play out in this space, bouncing off one wall, then another. Emptiness.

Sigh. Echoes of my sigh.

So here I am, in the very place where my end began.

The ceiling seems low, much lower than I recall. It has caved in a bit—perhaps because of the rainy season—and the walls seems flimsier. The shelves have started to decay, but are still laden with scrolls, most of which have crumpled to dust. Dust caught by a faint ray of light, dust traveling the air, dust settling down: on the floor, on the table, everywhere.

Twiddling his fingers after he has finished checking the thickness of the dust layer, Satan cannot help curling his lips in disgust. He seems to be obsessed with order.

"God," he says, "what an ugly mess!" And in spite of himself the wings come out, like swords out of their sheaths. Then they unfurl feather after feather, wave after frothy wave, till they are stuck there, nearly glued to the low ceiling.

Now his face is reddening.

"Don't you get excited again," I advise him. "You know it's not good for you."

No longer do I feel distraught. Instead—perhaps out of the force of habit, and the years of service as a housewife —I feel obligated to tidy up the place for him.

But as luck would have it, there are no cleaning supplies. So I tear the hem of my shroud and use it for a rag, and dust the chair so Satan may take his seat; which he does. His breath is regular again; and with a flap, the wings disappear.

I dust the long table, too; which is when the names Eliphaz the Temanite, Bildad the Shuhite and Zophar the Naamathite are suddenly unearthed. Like naughty schoolchildren, the three elders must have carved their names into the wooden surface, probably out of boredom. No wonder; prayer is no fun!

And then, then my eye falls upon something else, which is laid upon the table.

It is the only object here with no dust whatsoever. To my amazement, its leather cover seems utterly new, which makes my nostrils—what remains of them—flare: it smells fresh.

Has the book come into being just this moment? Conjured right here, under my nose, just for me? Shaken out of his wings, born out of thin air? How could I have missed it until now? Has it given no sound? No flip, no flap?

Am I dreaming? I stare at it in great awe.

"Ah!" says Satan, noting my expression with great interest. "You are a curious creature, woman."

"No disrespect intended, sir," I say, "but don't play with me. If you know my name—which I am sure you do—you would do well to use it when you talk to me."

"Oh, I would," he teases me, "if you were to offer me at least a token of gratitude, if you know what I mean."

I do. And it's not that I am not tempted... Satan is a handsome fellow, even with the fine-haired goat beard on his chin, which is something I could persuade him to shave off, in time...

"Here we are," he presses on. "All alone, apparently, in a deserted library... Now, how badly do you want your name back, woman?"

In place of an answer, I gulp.

And he says, "I am given to caprice, you know. So I may, perhaps, be persuaded to give your name back to you..."

His words go roundabout, but his gaze is quite direct. Which leaves me dumbfounded; but only for a second. After all, even as a corpse I cannot risk a scandal—and in my own village, or the copy of it, of all places! The place seems vacant at the moment—but then, who knows?

They say, walls have ears... And gossip, my God, it would be devastating. For sure, it would kill my husband.

His heart has been so weak lately. Betrayal—even a whisper of it—would crush him. It would add to the weight of his mounting woes. I still care for Job, even if I am here, trapped in this hellish replica of my birthplace, and he—somewhere up there, in the real thing.

In the silence that has fallen upon the room Satan leafs casually through the pages of the book. Then he raises the magnifying glass to his eye, and glares at me.

"I see," he says. "Didn't think so. Just testing; forget it."

"I will."

"You are not all that sexy, anyway."

"And you, sir, are not such a hotshot."

He raises his black eyebrows. "A dangerous thing to say to the Prince of Darkness," he says. "How did your husband take such insults?"

"Not well," I have to admit.

He licks his lips. "A devilish woman you are."

I nod as if to say, Perhaps I am.

Then, leaning in even closer to study the impact of his words upon me, his eyes come ablaze—or perhaps it is the sudden flash in the glass.

"Your demons," he says, "are inside."

Which this time, makes my voice falter. "Perhaps... Yes, perhaps they are. And you've said that before."

"I mean, they are here." He taps the cover of the book. "In these pages. Behold: this, you see, is the Book of Job."

I swallow hard. For a moment I cannot say a word.

Then, "Find it," I beg. "Find my words, if... If... I mean, if it's there—find what is left of my life, my so-called existence—"

"With pleasure," he says.

And without delay, he opens to the first page, and starts reading.

Then, "*In the land of Uz,*" he recites, looking straight through me, "*there lived a man whose name was Job. This man was blameless and upright; he feared God and shunned evil—*"

"Yeah, yeah," I say under my breath.

He raises a hairy eyebrow.

"The usual praise," I mutter, "whether Job deserved it or not... He has always been righteous in his own eyes—even when he sinned. Trust me, I am the one to know."

Satan ignores my grumbling and on he reads, "*He had seven sons and three daughters, and he owned seven thousand sheep, three thousand camels, five hundred yoke of oxen and five hundred donkeys, and had a large number of servants—*"

"And me?" I cannot help but cutting in. "What about me? Any mention of how he first laid eyes on me, how the fuck he got me pregnant, how on our honeymoon he took me to that hotel in Jerusalem—"

"Settle down, woman," says Satan. "This is not some cheap romance novel. And no, nothing about you; not a word so far."

"I see," say I. "Cattle is more important."

He gets up, and pop! One of his horns drives a hole in the ceiling.

"Don't interrupt me again, woman," he warns me. "I don't want to lose my temper. But you're quite right. The story is not too compelling, so far."

He turns a page or two and his face lights up. "Ah! Here starts the fun! Listen to this: *One day the angels came to present themselves before the Lord, and Satan also came with them. The Lord said to Satan, Where have you come from? Satan answered the Lord, From roaming throughout the earth, going back and forth on it.*"

"Your favorite phrase, I suppose."

He raises an eyebrow, then raises his voice over me. "*Then,*" he reads, "*the Lord said to Satan, Have you considered my servant Job? There is no one on earth like him; he is blameless and upright, a man who fears God and shuns evil—*"

And I say, "Like hell he is."

And he reads, "*Does Job fear God for nothing? Satan replied. Have you not put a hedge around him and his household and everything he has? You have blessed the work of his hands, so that his flocks and herds are spread throughout the land. But now stretch out your hand and strike everything he has, and he will surely curse you to your face.*"

And in a voice that is suddenly choked I say, "Lord in heaven... I know, now I know what happened. I know what you did to me."

And he counters, "Do you?"

"Yes," I say. And now, now the tears well up. "It's all because of you. What a calamity... The loss of my husband's property, his health.."

"Indeed," he says.

And with pride in his workmanship he goes on to prove me right. He quotes, with a clear tone of bragging, *"So went Satan forth from the presence of the Lord, and smote Job with sore boils from the sole of his foot unto his crown."*

Satan takes a pause, perhaps to study how I react, how I hang my head in shame.

"At first," I confess, "I couldn't feel much pity for Job. I suppose this is why I am punished here, in this realm, with boils on the soles of my feet."

"Perhaps so," says Satan. He seems quite amused.

I try to ignore the physical pain. I even bless it in my heart, because without heels, how can you hope to leave traces? My soul will drift away without these wounded soles, that serve to ground it.

Yes, they remind me that this is real. No, I cannot be dreaming. This place is more than a shadow of the other. In a strange way I am more alive now than ever.

Which brings out the other pain, the one I thought I had buried. It is smoldering now, burning me from the inside out.

"And then," I say, my voice barely heard, "then came the deaths. Our children... My seven sons, my three daughters... I won't...I can't tell you how devastated—"

I swallow my tears and struggle, somehow, to finish the sentence, "How broken I was, how consumed with grief... But to you—I can see it now—all this destruction, all this hurt is nothing, nothing but a bet —a move in a game."

And he corrects, "More like, a test case."

And awash with tears I stammer, I charge, "Is that what we are, sir, what our lives mean to you? Just some trick, a calculated battle maneuver, which you wish to analyze in hindsight, perhaps in preparation for a larger war?"

And he says, "Just so. How did you guess?"

"Men," I say, rolling my eyeballs.

And he recites, this time from memory, "Better to reign in Hell than to serve in Heaven."[1]

And I wonder, "Is it?"

He puts down the magnifying glass and glowers at me. "Woman, I am surprised at you! Don't you see it yet? No? You disappoint me, really! In a way—without even knowing it—you were helping me, advancing my cause."

"Was I?"

He turns a page, which has been earmarked, and from the top he quotes, *"Then said his wife unto him, Dost thou still retain thine integrity? Curse God, and die."*

"Yes," I say under my breath. "This I said."

"A clever woman you are! Job should have listened to you."

---

[1] A quote from Paradise Lost, by Milton

I shake my head, No. No.

"Had he cursed God, I would have won this bet, this maneuver, as you call it," he says. "Ah, sweet victory! How close it came to be! Too bad he denied you, denied me..."

"What did I do?" I ask, as if I were innocent.

"Woman, you must have known," says Satan, pointing at me, at the cavity around my heart, "you were my accomplice!"

"No," I refuse to agree with him. "I was feeling sorry for Job. My only sin, sir, is impatience. Anything —even death—is better than this hurt, this unrelenting torture. I wanted it to stop. Let it stop, stop already!"

"Don't lie to me now," he says. "The truth is simpler. You wanted to be free."

I turn my back on him and at once he rises from his seat. I hear the chair toppling over, and his step closing in, now directly behind me.

"You urged him to sin," says Satan. "And so, you have had enough. You wanted him to die."

"No, no, no!" I say.

"Oh well," he says. "You know I'm right. In this realm I can see to the hearts and guts of all inhabitants."

My hands on my ears I am trying hard not to hear him.

"Now listen, woman. If you admit your true intentions to me," he says, "I can reward you. I can give you what you want, and more."

Seeing the curiosity in my eyes, he goes on to offer, "First, your dream come true: I can let you have your name back. Then, imagine this: by my side, you can command power; lots of it. You can be my ally—or else, remain a poor, negligible soul. An empty shell, left to rot here, among the rest of them. Dust to dust."

I keep shuffling over the boils from one foot to another.

So slap! He closes the book, saying, "I shall give you little time to decide. So think, woman, think hard: who do you want to be? A dreamer—or one who acts, who takes the bull by its horns?"

"Don't know... I will be what I will be."[2]

"No human can become what he wills. Look at me: here I stand. Will you serve me? Will you bend to my will, and take command—right here by my side—of a new reality?"

"By your side?" I echo.

"Yes," he affirms. "By my side. Be mine, woman."

"Then," I reason, "in death as in life, it's a man's world. And so, my newfound position would come not from me, not from within. Nothing would change, really."

"Power," he emphasizes, as if this word alone were enough to tempt me.

It nearly is.

---

[2] In the bible, 'I will be what I will be' is the explicit name of God.

An unfamiliar resolve comes into my heart, and I realize: the moment is now. No need to torture myself. No more doubts. With great certainty, I know my answer. It is going to surprise him; hell, it surprises even me.

And so, raising my face to him, I declare, "I am what I am. With all my faults, all my weaknesses... I am," the words come easily now, they ring loud and clear, "Job's wife."

And I know that with this I am doomed to be lost here, with boils on my feet, forever on my quest.

The Hollow

She closed the book, placed it on the table, and finally decided to walk through the door. By now her eyes could barely stay open, and yet she knew, without having to look closely, that it wasn't a door really—only the opening for one. And over that threshold down there, she could somehow read the shape of the shadow. How it appeared suddenly, spilling out of nowhere, was quite beyond her, but she could tell, couldn't she, that there was no floor.

This time, perhaps because of starting to fall asleep, her diary seemed heavier than usual. Getting up, she brushed her fingers over it and could feel the raised spine, and rough spots where the gold lettering spelling '*Love*' had peeled off.

If she were to take it with her, the book might slip. It might drop from her hands. It might then continue dropping, farther and farther away from view through the empty elevator shaft, releasing letter after letter into the air, filling its darkness with white feathery pages, rustling, whispering what she had written such a long time ago, what had been clamped—until now—between the front and back covers, as if it were a flower meant for drying.

Her longing for him.

She wiped her face, and now her sight cleared. With every step toward that door, she could see his eyes shining brighter and brighter across from her, as if David—yes, as if he were right there, hanging in midair, framed by the hollow. By what twist of imagination did this happen? How did this outline of his jaw suddenly appear, how did it open now, as if he was just about to call her name?

In a moment, she thought, he would reach for her hand, smiling as if nothing bad could happen. And just like that last time, he would try to lead her over the scaffolding at the tenth floor of his newly erected skyscraper, with the blueprint rolled tightly under his arm.

She recalled: they had been married for ten years at the time of the accident. Since then, never once did she open her diary. Reluctant to decipher her own handwriting, which had looked different back then, more childish, she kept the book closed.

Let it all be forgotten: their first date, their wedding, honeymoon, because these memories would be followed—how could they not?—by that which had to be blocked: the image of him holding out his hand to guide her over, and the sound of his foot, stumbling.

But this morning, for some reason, she found the book open. How could that have happened? With a sudden shiver, she turned a page. To her surprise, that didn't bring back the sight of the void. This time the slanted sky, and the unstable earth below her—crisscrossed by metal poles and wooden planks—didn't rise up into view. There were no stains, even though she expected them to start spreading at that spot, far down below, where his body had come to its rest. She remembered his head giving a sharp tilt, which had been playing in her mind ever since, over and over and over again, as if he were just about to greet her. But to her amazement, this time there was no splutter.

Yes, a page must have turned...

So she closed her eyes, and brought back the last touch of his hand. It was as firm as ever. His fingers—she could almost feel them around her, all the way to the small of her back—his fingers gave her a sweet, strange feeling, which she had been missing for so long: the feeling of being home.

That was when, with a clap, she closed the book, then went through the missing door. With one easy step, which helped her ignore how final it was, she was flying, her hair pointing up, blowing wildly in the vertical wind. At first she avoided spreading open her arms, for fear of scraping them against the walls. Then, she heard her laughter, swirling loud and free, because there were no walls, only papery architectural designs around her. Sliding dreamily down, she was closer and closer to where she was headed all these years.

His kiss.

I, Woman

As told by a has-been slab of clay

I stand here before you, not knowing my name.

The light in this place is so blinding, so intense, that as far back as I can remember, it has forced me to close my eyes. Now this is about to change. Coming out of a brilliant haze, here is her footfall. Here she is: my Creator. I am clay in her hands. Let her do with me as she pleases; for what am I to do?

Now listen, listen to that sound: the air is vibrating around her. I can feel her breast, it is heaving. I can hear her breathing in, breathing out... Yes, she is coming closer. Is she about to blow life into me? My skin starts shivering. Here, now, is her touch—

She puts a mark on me, pressing the sharp end of a chisel until it stings, it pierces me right here, under my eyelid. I shriek! I cry—but somehow no one can hear me. If I were not reduced to tears, I would pay more attention to this nagging sense, the sense of astonishment in me. Why, why can't I be heard? Have I lost the ability to make a sound? Then I wonder, did I ever have it? And even in this crinkling, crushing silence, can't she sense my pain?

It is not until later, when she pulls out the blade, that I become afflicted—for the first time in my life—with vision. To you, vision may be a gift, but I think it a burden. Emerging from the glow that has so far pervaded my existence, I open my eyes.

The haze is gone. Alas, there is not much to see here around me. This is a dim place. A place of doubt. Clutter. Confusion. From this point on, I start sensing shadows. I find myself forced to make some sense of them.

So first, I spot her, the Creator. She is twice as tall as I am. With a heavy step, she paces around the space, coming in and out of my field of vision. Then, looking down, I spot that other presence, which in my blindness I could only guess. Him.

I used to imagine he was flat, a slab of clay. But now, to my surprise, he is no longer that. He, too, has risen from his slumber, yet he is not fully alive. Like me, he is immobile. At first glance he is blurry, gradually turning sharper and gaining more and more definition.

His hand is extended, as if to reach, to touch me. This, I figure, is a gesture of hope; which, out of spite, I may as well turn down. Being so close to him brings me too close to blushing, but I will never allow him to put a hand on me, and neither will she.

With a great deal of precision, the Creator coils a metal wire around the palm of his hand, loops it around and ties it to my fingers, fixing a small distance between us: clay, separation, clay. That way we are close—but not quite intimate.

From time to time, a slight vibration is transmitted from him. It comes through the coils, in a quiver that pierces me all the way through, right into the deepest parts of my flesh. The sound is, for lack of a better word, metallic. It sings about our pain, about the tension between us. I listen, and so does he. Weakness runs through our limbs, it twists in secret places inside us. He does his best to hold still, bravely maintaining his pose. And so do I.

The studio lights fall over him, casting shadow over shadow over the sharp, fragmented features of his face. They combine into a constantly changing countenance of definite indecision. Head tipped back in a most awkward manner, he seems to be straining, somehow, to look up at me. A sentence must have just died on his lips, for they are slightly parted.

Listen, I tell myself... Listen—can you hear?

But no. There is no breath left in him. Maybe there never was. So fragile, so irregular are his ribs that one of them, I think, may be missing.

He falls to his knees right here, at my feet, bending over backwards almost to the point of falling to pieces, and so, greatly straining every wire in his armature. His ankles are chained to a wooden base, where an assortment of chisels, pairs of pliers, sharp implements of every kind, wires thick and thin, hammers and nails are strewn in no apparent order, all around him. Am I chained, too? If so, I cannot tell.

Standing behind him on tiptoe, and leaning ever so lightly against his shoulder, I spread my arms. I feel entirely free—if not for these wires—to fly away. I have no need, I think, for this wooden base; nor do I find any use for this armature. I can tear out my ties. I can leave him. I can take wing! I can fly! Really, I am pretty sure I can.

And yet, it is my curiosity that will not allow me to do so.

For now that I am afflicted with vision, I appreciate how obscure things really are. The sharper the perception —the more complex the interpretation. There is nothing here, I tell myself: nothing but doubt. Every object is merely a shell, a container for so many uncertainties. And so I cannot help but wonder, Who am I? Did she make me in her image?

And who is he? What has happened here between us? What is our story? How will it unfold? How will it end? How much longer will we remain here, connected yet apart, suspended like this in frozen animation? And why, why are we in this place, at this particular moment? For whom are we posing?

Meanwhile, the Creator goes on to define me, curve by curve; tightening a wrinkle here, shaping a muscle there, carving my armpits, my wrists, my fingers, lifting and turning my head, polishing my skin, until—little by little, bit by bit—my body becomes silky smooth and my posture becomes light-footed, and ever more graceful.

And before long I sense a change. No longer am I clay; I am matter no more. Somehow, her touch has awakened a soul in me, teased a divinity out of dirt. I have become an icon, an embodiment of something larger. An eternal quality, an idea, more profound than Beauty, more lasting than Youth.

And so I find myself thinking, I am not an object. I am more than merely a figure. What I am is an idea:

I, Woman.

Can he name me? Can he guess who I am?

I whisper to him, I hint—I nag, even—but he is obstinately silent and furthermore, refuses to hear me. His head seems to hang down even lower than before; which may be explained, I tell myself, simply by the force of Gravity.

I call out to him. I signal in any one of my subtle ways —rising even higher on my tiptoe, stretching out my arms to snap his coils, pressing my weight into his back—but no matter how hard I try, he goes on giving me the same old, cold shoulder. Leaning against it, I stand there telling myself, Never mind. Let me forget how lonely I am. Let me try to amuse myself. So I invent different names for him. It is the name Adam he ignores most passionately.

Meanwhile she wields the chisel with great flare, gouging his body in several places, and excavating the sockets of his eyes. I know how it must feel. Throughout the process, his jaws remain tightly locked. He may be beside himself with the usual agony; he may be suffering from boredom; or both.

That night I hear, for the first time, a new noise. The noise of a crowd. People shuffling their feet, coughing, saying things they do not really mean.

"You're so talented! Such an inspiration," says a shrill voice just outside the studio.

"Oh, it's nothing," says the Creator, as if overcome, all of a sudden, by a sense of humility. "Lucky to walk and talk," she says, "just like the rest of us."

"Walk? Talk? Lucky you," grumbles a deep, melancholy voice from below.

Astonished, I turn my gaze to Adam. It could not have been him—now, could it? He seems so paralyzed, so restrained and so utterly focused on kneeling down in his particular shackled position as to have said absolutely nothing at all.

Meanwhile, she opens the door for the first guest. He offers numerous praises; which she accepts with a mix of visible pleasure and concealed distrust. I can tell she believes none of it—but all the same, praise, to her, is intoxicating. She can never get enough of it, which she will never admit, and which makes her angry with herself as well.

Now if you ask me, the guests are here for no other purpose than to pay tribute to me, as I rise over their heads in the flesh. Being in the nude, modesty has never been my strongest suit. Is it vanity, I ask you, to let them lay eyes on me, to delight in their cheers with such an open, shameless joy, and with no inhibitions whatsoever? Why should I refrain from basking in my own glory?

If you ask me, guilty pleasures are the only ones worth having.

More men come into the studio. Judging by the whistles and claps they do seem, at first blush, to revere me. They examine me all around: front to rear, top to bottom. My figure is so slender, my cheeks so voluptuous, and my bottom so round, that they have no choice but to adore me, and they do so tremendously. In particular, they hold my rump in high regard.

One of them shouts, "What an ass!"

The sentiment, I wish to tell him, is mutual.

But then, upon discovering the horribly disfigured figure at my feet, they tend to shrink away. I can feel them shuddering; yes, shuddering at the thought of coming face to face with their own mortality. I take a look at Adam, finding him in the worst of moods and as lost for words as ever.

Presently the women come in and start laughing at the poor devil. They peer into his vacant eyes, poke fun at his sunken cheeks, even yank at his chains, which makes him rattle on.

I feel so sorry for him. I wish to tell them, Enough! In this place, we are stuck—but not senseless! We are immobile—but not inanimate! We have feelings, for crying out loud!

My coils creak and at once, the women turn their attention to me; more precisely, to my supple breasts, which they seem to admire, and which inspire them to exchange information, detailed information about where to shop for some contraption called a bra. I figure, Oh well, they need support. If you look closely, everyone needs some kind of an armature.

Just then, a baby stumbles into the studio. The little one is so cute I could hug her, take her at once into my clay bosom, if only I were free to move. She points her pink little finger straight at my nipples, and cries hungrily, "Milk!"

Come here. Come to me, little one. Let me nurture you, I murmur. I, Woman.

Which is precisely the instant when, to my astonishment, Adam decides to come out of his silent stupor. And he does so with nothing less than pure poetry on his tongue. His eyes meet mine and then, with the deepest, most dramatic tones I have ever heard, he starts breathing out words:

From dust you gather me; I beg you on my knee

Look away... Imagine me, the way I used to be

Now shadows spread upon me, stain by stain

I shiver. Touch me, heal me; make me whole again[3]

Make you whole? Sure, I say, Why not! And finding myself aroused—which is quite easy in my state of undress —I tug at his strings as tenderly as I know how. To tell you the truth, I have a soft spot in me, when I think of him... I can truly feel it, deep inside. But then again, I cannot begin to imagine the way he used to be, and I am the last creature in the world to tell him that.

---

[3] This is the first verse of the poem *Dust* (immediately following *I, Woman*)

The next morning a broad shouldered man enters the studio and without troubling himself with a single word of introduction, he grabs the wooden base, upon which we stand, Adam and I. He lifts it, and hauls Adam and me out the door.

Meanwhile, the Creator puts on one of her shoes, and hobbles along the corridor after him, one heel clicking. "No!" she cries, in an unusually high pitch for her. "Stop! What do you think you are doing? Wait—"

He finds no need for explanation, and for her part she finds no reason to wait for one; for she immediately follows up with, "I told you to wait for me, didn't I? Yes I did. You forgot? It's no problem? I'm ruined. That's it! Enough! You're going to destroy them. I know you will. Too impulsive, is what you are. Reckless fool."

This bickering, so early in the day, is simply too much for me. So is this abrupt shake, as the man carries us over one final threshold, at which point we cross, quite sharply, from darkness to light.

I have never felt sunshine before—but all of a sudden it brings back a memory, a hazy memory of that glow, that blinding radiance that had pervaded my earlier, more innocent existence. At that moment I wish I could simply close my eyes and go back to being a slab of clay again.

"Careful! No... Slow down," she cries. "I swear, there will be nothing left of them by the time we get there. All thanks to you."

The man shrugs her off, which is a tricky thing to do while at the same time carrying the base, carrying us.

"Open the car," says he.

She takes her time to hop around, to put on her other shoe. Nothing is more urgent than the need to look your finest, I suppose.

"Hurry," he groans. "This thing is heavier than I thought."

She pulls out a handkerchief and wipes something under her lashes. Now I can see tears in her eyes and beads of sweat on his upper lip, both of which seem entirely unnecessary to me, for I can convey emotions more purely, through my pose alone, without all that excessive excretion. No need for tears and sweat.

The man bends down, sets us on the pavement and tries to catch his breath. As soon as the car door swings open, it becomes abundantly clear that the space inside may be too confined for Adam and me, not only emotionally speaking—but in a plain and literal sense, and that fitting us in is going to present a major challenge.

At first, great attention is given to the passenger seat. She covers it with a cloth and holds the door open as wide as mechanically possible, and possibly even wider.

He picks us up again, and proceeds to calculate his angle of approach into the car. Somehow, he succeeds in placing Adam and me halfway in—with our left hands spread out directly into the dashboard. It becomes clear that our right hands will not make it through the door without major damage to life and limb.

Together, they pull us out—coils humming—and start over. She retrieves the cloth, then spreads it again, this time over the backseat. He tilts the whole apparatus, quite precariously I might add, so it may clear the opening. I hold my breath, and so does Adam, but no one seems to notice.

The man pushes us in from the right, she pulls us in from the left. He controls, she contrives, a shout, a shriek, and the entire exercise is repeated, not once but at least three times, maybe more, using a different angle of approach each time, until—with carefully choreographed maneuvers, some heavy breathing and plenty of wangling —Adam and I find ourselves inside.

The mastermind behind the whole operation wipes his forehead, shuts the doors with a thud and starts the car. Meanwhile, the Creator steadies her nerves by clutching the armature to steady us. At the same time she tries to fix the wires that, one way or another, got bent out of shape.

Looking at the car window I notice that it bears my fingerprints, along with some other unidentified smudges of clay. Three of my delicate fingers have snapped off. I notice that Adam has them in the palm of his hand.

The wire that used to keep a measure of distance between us has snapped off, and thus, no longer do I have him wrapped around my finger. With every bump, every turn of the road, his head bounces back and forth. With unavoidable friction, Adam grazes up and down my waistline, leaving traces behind.

Our wires sing—but the tension that has been holding us together for so long is now less sound than before. So is the tension between them.

Her eyes are red, her face pale. I can feel her remorse. It pains her, certainly, that her man is in such a distress;

tears her up, practically. In short, it hurts her more than it hurts him, that it hurts him.

But trapped in her pride, she must now go on ignoring him the rest of the way—or at least until she can somehow extract an apology out of him.

After a long-winded drive, he brings the car to a stop near the entrance of a building, above which the sign, 'The Art Cast Foundry' is prominently displayed. The process of extricating Adam and me out of the car is as elaborate as can be imagined, if not more. There is a lot of pushing and pulling, shouting and crying, which helps us ignore the question of what is to come next.

How could we guess that which was clear to others: that our life—such as it is—is coming to an end; that these are our last moments together? Alas, had we known it, we would have taken a pause to cherish them. We would have attempted to take more pleasure in our pain.

But right now, there is no time for reflection. The man carries us up the stairs and into the building, and with every step, everything around us seems to be humming at a higher and higher pitch. Then, around the corner I am being greeted by several identical sisters, several bronze casts of the same sculpture.

The similarity between them is somewhat disquieting— but it inspires me to think of a new possibility: the possibility of being reborn, of living forever through multiple instances of myself. I wonder if such a rebirth can happen. I doubt it. Maybe it can, but then—at what cost to me? At what degree of pain?

The fluorescent light falls upon the busts of these sisters with a steely shine, quite unlike the way it washes over me. Set upon slippery marble pedestals, they look at me with a superior attitude. Miraculously they are unchained by any wires, unconnected to any armature. Indeed, they are free—but their freedom must have come at the cost of becoming hard. I can see it in their eyes. So, on the way past them I laugh in their faces. It is clear to them, is it not, that they are merely copies, and I—the original.

Meanwhile, we are brought into the inner space. Here, a display of patina samples hangs on the wall, as well as a number of shelves piled high with molds and empty shells, which they use for casting. A smell of molten wax is in the air. A tiny flame and its reflection, separated by a thin line, are burning there. Together, they shed flickering lights across the huge, metallic table. The closer I come, the more alarming I find it.

The surface, quite eerily, brings to mind a battlefield scene: it is crisscrossed with cutting tools, and laden with twisted bodies, dismembered limbs. At once, Adam recoils in horror. It hurts me to see him so shaken. He spreads his hands out—his usual position—in a mute call for help. But to no avail, for it is upon this surface that, finally, the man sets us down.

"There," he says as he turns to leave the room, "Take a last look."

The Creator spins the base around, inspecting us for any bumps and bruises from the long ride and fixing when necessary. Meanwhile, new people come in and stand there, waiting.

"You need anything?" one of them asks, hinting at the cutting tools.

"No," says the Creator, tersely.

She wipes the traces, the clay traces left unwittingly by Adam all around my waistline. She adjusts my back, neck and head. Lastly, she sticks the three missing fingers back in place.

"That's it," she says. "I'm done."

And with that she, too, disappears from view. Will she be coming back?

I am patient. I wait for her. I search for a hint, a breath, a touch—only to realize that waiting is pointless. We have been abandoned.

The Creator has turned us over, unceremoniously and with no parting words, into the hands of strangers. For what reason? What will they do with us? How long do we have? There must be some purpose to this suffering... Is there?

Adam looks at me more tenderly than ever. We cling to each other, clay to clay. The silence between us screams fear.

Now they turn on a big kiln, pick up their tools and, one by one, come over to surround us. They snip at the coils and break Adam free. I can see only a glimpse of him between their shoulders. He strains, in his own quiet manner, to give me one last look. They lift him away, after which I lose sight of him forever.

I can remember very little after that. The light in this place is so white, so intense, it fills me with such radiance that I am forced to close my eyes. The air is hot, and getting hotter, and yet I can feel a shiver running through me. Something is changing here, inside and out. The Creator is coming. She is near me, around me. I have no doubt.

A big flame of fire flares up, engulfing me. I feel it in my veins, swelling in me like a flow of molten bronze. I hear it in the crackling of embers from below. That hazy glow of my earlier existence is finally here, burning brighter than ever.

I am grateful to go back. No longer am I stuck here, in a place of doubt.

No longer am I inflicted with sensing shadows. Ashes to ashes. Dust to dust. All my sorrows are about to melt away. In this inferno, nothing will be left behind me but an empty shell. I fly into the brilliance. I am ablaze. I am in bliss. For where I am going I shall be reborn.

Dust

He:

From dust you gather me

I beg you on my knee

Look away—imagine me,

The way I used to be

Now shadows spread upon me

Stain by stain

I shiver. Touch me, heal me

Make me whole again

She:

I see him in my mind

He moves, he stirs tonight

But when I come to him,

Our limbs entwined

That arm wraps around me

It holds me and controls me—

Can we take flight?

Twisted

He:

In darkness take a leap

For trust is blind

Imagine me: I'll lift you,

Caress you and possess you

Imagine us:

In passion and in sweep

Our limbs entwined

She:

Pressed against that ribcage

Where not a breath escapes

Not a sigh of sorrow,

Not a cry of rage

How can I bear his silence

When shadows grow immense—

He:

If shadows peel and lift away

If ever you break free

From my embrace

If you catch sight of me

In light of day—

Go... Leave me here,

My grace,

In my debris—

Uvi Poznansky

She:

In my dream I'm soaring

Amidst a flap of wings

My heart so light,

So happy,

Forgetting him, ignoring

That arm

Wrapped around me,

How heavily it clings

Twisted

He:

Go!

My spirit crushed and humble

No feeling left, no lust

Abandoned here

To crumble...

Not strong enough to blow

These fading marks

Of footfalls,

Your footfalls, off my dust

She:

I will not let you blur

These traces in my mind

Of the way we were

Our limbs entwined

I miss you, still resist you,

Forgive me, for I must

Gather you so gently

From the dust.

The Art of Dust I

The Art of Dust II

The One Who Never Leaves

She sits at the edge of the crooked old couch, knees pressed tightly together, and I can sense a little tremor traveling up her spine. I try to calm her down, which is to say, I clear my throat, after which I proceed to explain to her—in my softest, most polite tone—that contrary to popular belief, feline creatures do not have nine lives.

She stares at me, terrified.

As well she should be. Yes, both of us know, all too well: she is the stranger around here. She would be gone before the day is over. I am the one who never leaves.

"Really," I insist, over her silence. "There's no such thing as nine lives."

She leans back, sinking deeper and deeper into the frayed cushion, not doing much of anything except breathing heavily. Naturally, it annoys me. Hell, it sucks the air out of my lungs. The danger of oxygen deprivation does not occur to me at first. But if there is one thing I have come to hate more than her breathing heavily, it is me, having to hold my breath.

So many months have passed since I smelled fresh air. Come to think of it, it must have been years since I crossed the threshold, since I stepped outside, into the sunlight, which—as I remember—is so warm, so gloriously magnificent. Yes, it must have been decades since I sunk my paws into the moist ground outside, or lifted my eyes to the blue sky, or chased birds. I remember how, having caught them, I would ruffle their feathers, and lick their throats ever so playfully.

Being locked here I have managed to squash these memories. I have grown quite resigned, somehow, to the stale perfume rising here, from these blankets, which she now gathers around her.

Trust me, I don't miss the fresh air anymore. Out of boredom I have lost the urge to prowl around this place, from one room to another. All I do is groom my tail, which is a sorry sight, because the limp thing has lost most of its hair by now. There is only one small clump of fuzz, clinging by a thread to its very end. I brush around it ever so gently, then lick my fangs, which have become somewhat dull lately. I find the hairline cracks in them, polish them with my tongue, ponder the perils of old age, and try to stay calm, keeping my eye on her.

True, her scent is overwhelming, her heartbeat palpable, her presence inescapable. In spite of my best intentions, she makes me hate her. Yet, she draws me in. I am focused on her as if she were my prey, and she knows it.

I ignore the chirping of birds, drifting in through the windows—yet the taste of their flesh fills my mouth. They flap, flap, flap their wings out there... So darn free, so delectably fluffy! And here I am. I try to pay no attention to that immensely heavy key, hanging way out of reach up there on a rusty nail, by the main door. Why should I.

I never show weakness. And most certainly, I never meow.

"You know cats," I say. "Just one short, miserable life, that's what they have. Interrupted, every so often, by having to beg strangers... Can you imagine? Really, I have to beg them for the most basic needs."

I find it difficult to guess if she believes me.

"My life, if you can call it that, may soon be over. I'm hungry. I could die. Really," I stress to her.

She just sits there, and the window behind her shows her reflection; and her reflection is paralyzed, too. I can see a green flash of anger in the glass, and by hook and by crook I know, without thinking twice, what she sees in my eyes.

"I'm dying here!" I growl, "Food! Something to eat!"

And for added emphasis I arch my back. She may take that as a threat, but I assure you, for me it is nothing more than a sudden urge to stretch.

Somehow the sight of my sharp claws brings her to her senses, and so she removes the blankets in a big hurry. She has—or rather, used to have—a pretty figure, I conclude, now that I see it. The fabric is swishing softly as she ties the belt around her waist, showing off that which was once slender, but now is merely fragile.

I trot behind her to the kitchen, and watch in amazement as she fumbles about, opening and closing cabinet doors in utter confusion. By now, I am deeply in despair. Something fizzles in my throat, but I do my best to hold back, to subdue it from becoming a full-throated hiss.

"What's the fuss?" I ask. "Did I ask you to catch mice? Look here, for crying out loud, look inside already!"

And with that, I thread my long, flexible tail directly into the handle of the pantry door. It gives way, it opens with the usual creak, and there, on the lowest shelf, is that thing I learned to crave: A can with a lovely whiskered face on it.

She picks it up. I wait. I do not meow.

Now she embarks on shuffling stuff in the drawer. The hunger grows in me as the clink and the clank rise higher and higher, as spiky and prickly as rage. Finally she digs out a shiny tool and then, snap! She sticks it into the thing, right there between those whiskers.

And with that one blow, the aroma! Ah, tinged with blood, it spreads instantly, all over the place. Is she a killer, I ask myself. Is she is a killer, too?

Full of awe, I watch her closely as she labors to cut the thing open. I study her from one side, then from the other, only to catch her shooting a little glint at me from the corner of her eye. I can see that she is calculating, with a little smile, the twisting of her knife.

Alas, in this place, my hunger puts me at her mercy. So she is using this particular moment, I figure, to play a cruel game with me, a game of measure for measure: a measure of her skill with the knife against the measure of the pain in my stomach. Her power against my need.

Her lips curl up, as if to say, Let me hear you purr, will you? No?

Her skin hangs under her chin and around her neck like a delicate necklace, wrinkle upon wrinkle, and her face is fallen. I can, without too much effort, use my bad eye to erase—if only for a squint—the marks of time on her. For that brief second I find in her the playful, if not innocent, face of a kitten.

"What happened? You swallowed your tongue?" she asks teasingly. "You're as quiet as a mouse!"

My stomach growls, so I just crouch there, staring helplessly at her knife.

"This place," she casts a look around her. "Oh my, it gave me the creeps at first. I mean, no one told me it came not only with furniture, but with a pet, too."

In place of an answer I claw her leg, because hell, I am more than some useless old nicknack. Beware. I am dangerous.

So to sooth me, she goes, "Oh my, such an adorable tail! I love it, I do!"

And I go, "No you don't. You hate me, but not half as much as I hate you... Food! Quick, miss," I hiss. "I'm dying here!"

Perhaps she gets what I say, because now she heaps the food on a plate and then, at long last, sets it before me. I tear into it. I lick the plate clean. I pass my tongue over my paws. I wipe my whiskers clean.

But I never meow.

I hop onto the counter. She has left the knife here, so I inch closer, just to sniff it—but then, the sight of whiskers from the metallic surface makes me cautious.

Wait, where is she now? Oh, there! Beating a full retreat, she is making her way back to the couch. I come closer, rubbing myself against her feet, as happy and bushy-tailed as I allow myself to be. I feel stronger now. Bushy-tailed or not, the clump of fuzz is about to fall off my rear end—but in spite of this I feel invincible.

With the single exception of the main door, which is locked, there is no door here I cannot push open. She knows it. She knows there is no point in hiding from me.

I glance at the window. Between the smudges and through the layers of dust, fragments of murky sky are getting darker. I curl up beside her, rub against her skin for warmth and, with my eyes nearly closed, I rock my head to and fro with a long, sweeping motion. These days, there is nothing I like better than licking myself.

She shrinks away, while at the same time making pronounced efforts to ignore me.

With every instinct in me I know one thing for sure: despite her silence, which is an insult to my pride; despite her looking away in every possible direction, at this corner then the other; and despite the failing light, she can still see me—or at least my eye, the good one, shining at her from the darkness.

So at the end of an unbearably drawn out, tense second, here it is: she gives a jerk—a sharp one, mind you! And with a click, she brings in a host of shadows by turning on the twisted lamp by her side.

What do I care? I am busy, trying to imagine sun. Curling around myself, eyes half-open, I pass my tongue around my fangs. Here, it is coming to me: a radiant, blood-red sun. Sky—ground—birds—flap, flap, leap!—throats—

I feel her looking at me, trying, perhaps, to decipher the sudden flash in my slit pupils. I flick her with my tail. The shadows—small and large, sharp and fuzzy—all flick their tails at her.

I am the master of this place! I am the one who never leaves. She will be gone before this day is over.

Then I will be cold. I will be alone once more. Locked. Helpless. Choked to tears by something quite inexplicable. Perhaps that stale perfume. Or else, the fading of that stale perfume. And I know: in vain will I resist staring at that immensely heavy key, hanging way out of reach, up there on that rusty nail, by the main door.

But never will I meow.

About This Book

In this unique collection, discover diverse tales, laden with shades of mystery. Come into a dark, strange world, a hyper-reality where nearly everything is firmly rooted in the familiar— except for some quirky detail that twists the yarn, and takes it for a spin in an unexpected direction. So prepare yourself: keep the lights on.

Inspired by the author's art and by literature, these tales come from different times and places, with characters that search for their identity and challenge their hellish fate. Yet all of them share one thing in common: an unusual mind, one that is twisted.

About the Author

U vi Poznansky is a *USA TODAY* bestselling, award-winning author, poet and artist. "I paint with my pen," she says, "and write with my paintbrush."

Uvi earned her B. A. in Architecture and Town Planning from the Technion in Haifa, Israel. During her studies and in the years immediately following her graduation, she practiced with an innovative Architectural firm, taking part in the design of a large-scale project, Home for the Soldier.

Having moved to Troy, N.Y. with her husband and two children, Uvi received a Fellowship grant and a Teaching Assistantship from the Architecture department at Rensselaer Polytechnic Institute. There, she guided teams in a variety of design projects and earned her M.A. in Architecture. Then, taking a sharp turn in her education, she earned her M.S. degree in Computer Science from the University of Michigan.

During the years she spent in advancing her career—first as an architect, and later as a software engineer, software team leader, software manager and a software consultant (with an emphasis on user interface for medical instruments devices)—she wrote and painted constantly. In addition, she taught art appreciation classes.

Her versatile body of work can be seen in two websites: her blog includes thoughts about the creative process, reader reviews, author interviews, excerpts from her novels, voice clips from her audiobooks, poems and short stories. Her art site includes bronze and ceramic sculptures, paper engineering projects, oil and watercolor paintings, charcoal, pen and pencil drawings, and mixed media.

Coma Confidential, Overkill, Overdose, and Overdue are novels in the Ash Suspense Thrillers with a Dash of Romance series. With each new case, Ash uses grit and intuition to solve the crime.

Virtually Lace is the first volume in a multi-author thriller series, High-Tech Crime Solvers, where the authors bring each other's characters into their books.

My Own Voice, The White Piano, The Music of Us, Dancing with Air, and Marriage before Death are novels in the Still Life with Memories series, a family saga with a love story that develops in the face of hardship and illness over two generations, starting at the 1980's, then harkening back to WWII when Lenny, a soldier, and Natasha, a rising star, first met. These books are also offered in two bundles: Apart from Love and Apart from War.

Rise to Power, A Peek at Bathsheba, and The Edge of Revolt are novels in The David Chronicles, telling the story of David as you have never heard it before: from the king himself, telling the unofficial version, the one he never allowed his court scribes to recount. In his mind, history is written to praise the victorious— but at the last stretch of his illustrious life, he feels an irresistible urge to tell the truth. These books are also offered in a trilogy.

In addition, The David Chronicles includes six art collections: Inspired by Art: Fighting Goliath, Inspired by Art: Fall of a Giant, Inspired by Art: Rise to Power, Inspired by Art:

A Peek at Bathsheba, Inspired by Art: The Edge of Revolt, and Inspired by Art: The Last Concubine.

A Favorite Son, a new-age twist on an old yarn, is inspired by the biblical story of Jacob and his mother Rebecca, plotting together against the elderly father Isaac, who is lying on his deathbed.

Twisted is a unique collection, laden with shades of mystery. Here, you will come into a dark, strange world, a hyper-reality where nearly everything is firmly rooted in the familiar—except for some quirky detail that twists the yarn.

Home and Can We Still Love, Uvi's deeply moving poetry books in tribute of her father, include her poetry and prose as well as translated poems from the pen of her father, the poet, author and artist Zeev Kachel.

Uvi wrote and illustrated two children's books, Jess and Wiggle and Now I Am Paper. Watch the beautiful animations she created for these books on YouTube.

About the Cover and Artwork

A few months ago, a pile of bones captured my fascination. Scattered across my desk, they were ashen, rather small, and of fanciful shapes. I was unable to identify the animals whose remains these were, nor could I name their skeletal parts. Which left me free to mine—out of these crumbling, fragile relics—an entirely new presence. Coming to life on brown paper with with a few stokes of white, red, and brown pencils, there she was: my Bone Princess.

Set upon a patch of scorching desert sand, she casts a one-eyed look at you, which masks how vulnerable she really is. Her soft flesh is shielded—and in places, nearly crushed—by her armor of bones. She is damaged: no arms, no legs, yet she accepts her pain with pride, and with regal grace. Inside and out, she carries a sense of morbidity.

As all creations, she became an independent spirit. As such, she made me wonder what had happened to her. I imagined her turning to me, curving the elegant, elongated lines of her neck, to tell me her story. This was how my novella, the first one in this collection—*I Am What I Am*—came to be.

Twisted.

*

To illustrate the connection between the poem *Dust* and the story *I, Woman*, I included two photographs in this book. Together, these photographs suggest the transition a piece of art undergoes in the foundry.

- One photograph shows my nearly completed clay model (still in my studio, where the armature holds it in place) for a sculpture of two dancers. The sculpture is titled *Can We Take Flight*.

- The other photograph shows my finished bronze sculpture titled *From Dust*. Having been fired, its armature is no longer necessary and has been removed.

In each photograph, the dancers strike a different pose, which represents a verse in my poem *Dust*. The poem, which comes directly from their lips, is a duet describing a love-hate tension in their relationship.

When the sculpting process takes several labor-intensive months, an intimate feel develops between me and the clay. So much so that the dancers come alive even before I place the last mark on them. They start having a voice, describing not only their finished state, but the process, the change they undergo, starting at the studio and ending at the kiln.

"I stand here before you, not knowing my name..."

So starts one of the strangest stories I have ever written... Having witnessed the casting process—which takes as long as six weeks from the time the clay model

arrives at the foundry and a bronze sculpture is made—
made me think of death and rebirth, which is the theme of
my story *I, Woman*.

Uvi Poznansky

A Note to the Reader

T hank you for reading this book! I hope you enjoyed it. I invite you to check out more books from the same pen. There is always a new project on my drawing board, so come back to check it out.

I would love to hear what you thought of this book. You have the power of bringing it to the attention of more readers, by posting your own review. It would mean so much to me.

And another thing you can do to help me spread the word is this: please tell your friends about my work. How else will they hear about the story? How else will the characters, who sprang from my mind onto these pages, leap from there into new minds?

Bonus Excerpts
Excerpt: The Music of Us

My son, Ben, has been gone for a month now, staying in some youth hostel in Rome. If I call him, if I stumble into revealing how scared I am that his mother is losing her mind, he may listen. He may heed my fears, grudgingly, and come back here, not even knowing how to offer his support to me. Should I ask for it?

The last thing I wish to do is lean on him for help. He is not strong enough, and whatever the problem may be with her, I can grit my teeth and handle it, somehow, all by myself. Besides, I pray for a spontaneous change in her. I mean, her memory may take a turn for the better just as quickly as it has deteriorated.

Given this hope I decide that for now I will not schedule the head X-Ray that her doctor recommended for her. I figure she has been through so many checkups, so many exams to rule out depression, vitamin B deficiency, and a long list of other possible ailments, all of which has been in vain.

So far, the results have failed to produce a conclusive diagnosis, and this new X-Ray will be no different, because from what I have read, Alzheimer's disease can be determined only through autopsy, by linking clinical measures with an examination of brain tissue. So this new medical hypothesis is just that: a hypothesis. One that cannot be proven; one that cannot go away. An ever-present threat.

Perhaps all she needs is rest. Time, I tell myself. I must give her time. Meanwhile I resolve to keep her condition secret from everyone, especially from my son. Let him enjoy his time away from home, his independence.

Since his departure I called him only once, three weeks ago, and said little, except for blurting out the mundane, "How's Rome?"

"Great," he said vaguely, adding no particulars.

I could not help myself from asking. "So, what about your plans?"

"What about them?"

"D'you have any?"

"For now I have none," he admitted, and immediately changed the subject. "How's mom?"

"Fine."

"Is she?"

"She is," I lied, hoping that the sound of my voice would not betray the tensing of my muscles, the tightening of my jaws.

"Oh good," he said. "Really, really good."

There is only one thing more difficult than talking to Ben, and that is writing to him. Amazingly, having to conceal what his mother is going through makes every word—even on subjects unrelated to her—that much harder. I find myself oppressed by my own self-imposed discipline, the discipline of silence.

And what can I tell him, really? That I keep digging into the past, mining its moments, trying to piece them together this way and that, dusting off each memory of Natasha, of how we were, the highs and lows of the music of us, to find out where the problem may have started?

To him, that may seem like an exercise in futility. For me, it is a necessary process of discovery, one that is as tormenting as it is delightful. If the dissonance in our life would fade away, so will the harmony.

Sometimes I go as far back as the moment we first met, when I was a soldier and she—a star, brilliant yet illusive. Natasha was a riddle to me then, and to this day, with all the changes she has gone through, she still is.

I often wonder: can we ever understand, truly understand each other—soldier and musician, man and woman, one heart and another? Will we ever again dance together to the same beat? Is there a point where we may still touch?

Excerpt: Dancing with Air

Overcome, suddenly, by exhaustion, Natasha stepped out of my embrace and plopped onto her suitcase. "Ma came to say goodbye, " she said. "I saw her across from me, as we left the shore. She was offering a prayer, tears running down her cheeks. Then, once out to sea, the Germans fired at us."

"Really? What happened?"

"The ships, they took up their positions in the convoy and plodded ahead. Straightaway, two of them were lost. One ran aground. The other, suffering from engine trouble, turned back to the harbor. And as for us I thought that was the end."

I shuddered at the thought.

"This journey," said Natasha, "it was more challenging than anything I've gone through in the past. Even watching Papa during his last months was easier, in a way, because back then I was on the outside, observing his pain."

I waited for her to continue.

After a slight reflection, she added, "I could only guess what was happening to him, I mean, the ways his illness drained his mind, the ways he suffered. But now, I wasn't an observer. I lived it, Lenny! Everyone on board—including me—was going through the same fear, the same hardship."

I could not help but ask her, "What were you thinking, putting yourself at risk?"

In reply, she rose to her feet. "For this very moment," she said, clinging to me, "I would go through it all over again."

I took a step back, to stress, "Your Mama, she's beside herself with worry, and as for me—"

"You talked to her?" asked Natasha, her eyes twinkling. "Of course you did, how else would you know to wait here for me? She doesn't get it—"

"And neither do I!"

"But Lenny, it's so simple! I missed you—"

"That's no reason, Natasha, for what you've done. Why leave home, especially now, when we're at war? If you love me, keep yourself safe, if only for my sake! Why, why put your life at risk —"

"Perhaps," she said, "I'm not looking for safety! Have you ever thought of that? Perhaps something else is more important to me."

"Like what?"

"I can't continue to depend on others, Lenny, the way I've done all my life. This is my time to change, to demand new things of myself, even if they happen to frighten me, even if I'm scared out of my mind."

"Not sure I understand—"

"Please try, Lenny."

"What is it you want?"

"Just this: to stop leaning on those closest to me."

"You could've done that back home, couldn't you?"

"That's the place where I'm being taken care of, to the point of feeling stuck. Worse than that: suffocated. Someone, usually Mama, drives me to where I need to be. Someone points me to the dressing room, calls me to the stage. I'm nothing more than a mechanical doll. All I do is respond."

"You do much more than that! You excite audiences, Natasha! And to me, you're an inspiration—"

"Yes, you admire the way I play, but in truth music is the only thing for which Papa trained me."

"You're too critical of yourself," I said.

To which she said, "No, Lenny. I've seen him decline, seen him lose his mind, and if—if, like him, I'll ever lose mine—how in the world will I recover? How will I find my way, when I've never developed the skill to do so?"

I lowered my head before her.

"Never," I said, "until now."

"Exactly," said Natasha. "Until now."

And a moment later, blotting the corner of her eye, where a tear was forming, she whispered to me, "Come closer, Lenny, snuggle up, but never, ever let me lean on you."

Excerpt: Marriage before Death

Without uttering a sound I gave her a look, begging her to leave. Rochelle gave one to me, begging me to play along.

Out loud she said, "Oh how I hate you! I hate you now more than I ever loved you!"

At that, the SS officer burst out laughing. It lasted quite a while, or so it seemed to me, and by the time it finally ended, a cruel smile was left across his face, stretching from one pointy ear to the other.

"*Ach*," he hissed. "What a woman! Cold one minute—hot the next!"

Rochelle hung her eyes on me one more time.

"At the very least," she implored, "you should say you are sorry, so sorry to have left me in such a difficult situation!"

The SS officer cut in.

"Didn't I tell you?" he asked her. "His kind, they have no morals! Worse than animals is what they are."

She turned away and went back to his side. From there she said, in a tone of regret, "Right you are. I was naive, up to now, to hope for anything different from him."

Over her sorrow, the SS officer went on to say, "How could you ever let yourself be seduced by such a man?"

She shook her head. "How silly of me! How foolish it is to hope! I was sure he would confirm to everyone here his desire to marry me."

To which the SS officer said, "Now, mademoiselle, you have learned your lesson."

She gave him a tearful smile, but then could not help crying out to me, "Oh, for heaven's sake, don't you get it? I'm expecting your child!"

At that I had a change of heart. Why? First, because I was moved to tears by her plea, no matter if it was a fake one or not; and second, because what had I got to lose?

So I uttered, "Forgive me, Rochelle."

"What?" she asked. "What did you say?"

"Forgive me," I said, with a catch in my throat. "If I were a free man I would gladly keep my promise to you."

A triumphant smile played on her red lips. Yet, for just a moment, she was silent.

I thought she might make peace with me, now that I relented. Instead, she turned to the SS officer.

"Herr Müller," she said. "I'm not here to beg for mercy for this man."

In surprise, "You're not?" he asked, raising a thick eyebrow.

And from the other side of the table, his French collaborator echoed, "You're not?"

My face was still burning, still stinging from that slap of hers. I bit my lips to overcome the pain. If I could muster the nerve to speak up once more, I would ask her the very same thing.

Really? You're not?

"No," she stressed.

The toothbrush mustache under Herr Müller's nose started to twitch. Perhaps he was becoming suspicious of her.

"I thought," he said, "that you had a big favor to ask of me."

And she said, "I do."

And he said, "Well? What is it, then?"

"For the sake of my family," said Rochelle, "for the pride of my father, for my own honor, and for the future of this baby, I cannot be an unwed mother! I'd rather die!"

Becoming somewhat impatient, "*Ach!*" he said. "You should have thought of that earlier, before you got involved with the likes of him."

It was then that she said, "I promise, Herr Müller, giving me what I ask for is sure to give you the greatest pleasure, because it is just what this man deserves."

"Which is what?"

"Marriage before death."

Excerpt: Coma Confidential

R hythms of footfalls are intensifying outside my hospital room. It must be morning. Immobile, all I can' do is count beats. I must have spent days here—who knows, maybe even weeks—or else I wouldn't be able to tell time by means of listening to echoes.

It's a new skill, a new gain for me, barely significant enough to offset the loss of something far more important: my identity. Even so, I'm proud. I pat myself on the back. Mentally.

By their patter, I know that two pair of shoes have just stepped into the room. It doesn't take much to figure who is standing in them. The two nurses prattle about having to change my feeding tube. In a blink, a craving comes over me.

Oh, what I would give for a decent donut! I drool at the thought of dunking it into a bowl filled with smooth, warm, vanilla-flavored sugar glaze, then lifting it to my mouth for a quick lick.

One of the nurses wipes the dribble off my chin. I wish she would stop handling me. I wish I could turn my head away.

Meanwhile, my stomach is growling. I'm so hungry. At this point, never mind pastry. I'll take any real food—even peas and carrots, which normally I hate. Being able to chew them would cast me back among the living.

In this sorry state, I've come to acquire a new affinity with vegetables. Maybe they have feelings, too. Maybe they dread being poked about with a fork, just as much as I fear being injected. Maybe being sucked down that dark, cavernous windpipe to be consumed by something yet unknown is repulsive to them. I think that at long last, I understand carrots and peas. So no, I'm never going to put them in my mouth again.

Seriously, I prefer donuts.

"Oh my! Accident?" asks one nurse, while pumping liquid food into my stomach with a syringe.

"No, worse than that," says the other one. By comparison, her voice is lower and more mature. It is also secretive.

"What can be worse than an accident?"

"Don't even ask."

"Fine, then. Let's talk about something else."

"Like what?"

"Like, what d'you want to be, ten years from now?"

There's a faint sound—maybe the older nurse is scratching her head—which leaves the question unanswered. Oh, the things I'd say, if only I could revive my vocal cords! I'd shout, "Ten years, are you kidding me? Who cares! I just want to make it through today!"

But on second thought, I want more than that, much more. I strain my vocal cords in a desperate attempt to cry out, "I want to wake up from this nightmare, at the snap of my fingers. I want to walk away from this bed. Most of all, I want to know who I am. Is that too much to ask?"

Excerpt: Overkill

E d lies still on the sidewalk, his eyelids open but unflinching. The only thing about him that moves are the lapels of his corduroy coat, flapping slightly this way and that across his neck as the wind floats chilly feelers over his body.

Timmy gasps—but his eyes are not tearful, not yet. In that second, when time slows, the driver side door is swaying with an annoying noise. With each squeak, the child takes a gulp of air as if about to ask, "Dad, will you get up? Will you grab the door handle?"

No blood is visible, at first. So, I too allow myself to wonder: Will Ed climb back into his seat, dust off his shoulders, and wave goodbye to his son, before driving away?

I expect him to do so. Almost.

Until another round of gunshots blasts the air.

Without even thinking, I push Timmy down to the asphalt, which is quite easy because he's such a skinny child and utterly in shock. Then I land hard on my elbows beside him and push a hand against his chest until he crawls backwards, until he butts against his father's car. It casts a shadow over him. At the moment, there is no better place to hide.

Up on the pavement, a short distance from us, blood starts puddling around Ed's shoulder. I try to block Timmy from seeing it.

He shakes his head, still in disbelief.

Please, God, no. This can't be true.

Everything around us is in a state of utter confusion. The sidewalk is strewn with abandoned backpacks, as some pupils are running for their lives. Others cower behind a bush or a car. One uses his flimsy umbrella as a shield.

A teacher cries out to him, "Duck!"

And another teacher, by the gate of the school, yells, "Run! Get inside! Get down, crawl under your desks! And for Heaven's sake, stay away from the windows!"

A couple of parents attempt getting out of their cars to pull their children to safety, but at the sound of shooting they drop to their knees with empty arms.

Next to me, Timmy turns onto his stomach, mashes his nose against the tire, and wedges himself, somehow, between the curb and the Ford. Then he crawls under it toward the rear bumper, making room for me, too.

I try to cock my head up from the damp surface. Looking at the scene from under the belly of a car is a whole different experience. Someone stands at the other side of the car, and all I can see is his sneakers, socks, and the hem of his coat, flaring at its bottom. Also, the muzzle of his gun. For a heartbeat, before dark clouds close in, it glints in the sunlight.

I reach over and clamp a hand over Timmy's mouth to prevent him from screaming, from drawing the killer's attention. A hail of bullets rains down, sparking off the front bumper.

Timmy tenses up. His breath trembles as it escapes my touch. I must protect him. I must bring him back safely to his mother.

The edge of the curb gouges into my back. I adjust, I turn over. Now it presses against my belly.

I must not lose this child, either.

Now, the killer kicks the grill of the car, then jams his weapon, hard, into the front window. I know it by seeing only one of his feet on the ground and by the sound of cracking. It reverberates all over as the car shakes. Shards of glass come pinging against the asphalt and stab at my fingers.

Why is he wasting his time—at the risk of being identified, or even caught—on an empty car, when all around us, juicier targets come into his view?

Excerpt: Virtually Lace

E ven before Michael spotted the body, the idea of creating a simulation of the scene occurred to him. At sunset, the panoramic view of Laguna Beach was awe-inspiring. He wondered if he could render it convincingly in his model, the virtual reality model which he had been developing in the back of his garage for months, until the recent acquisition of his software by a military ops company.

Could beauty be taken apart without loss of emotional impact? Could its data be synthesized, somehow, into a lifelike experience? In short, could he apply his analytical skills to fool his own senses?

For now, these were purely academic questions. They occupied his mind, which helped him forget his loneliness. Michael brought his car to a stop at the corner of Cliff Drive and let it maneuver by itself into a tight parking spot. In all probability, this evening would be uneventful, or so he thought. It was the end of April. He had nothing to do and no one to do it with.

Sitting there awhile, lost in his thoughts, how was he to know that in the coming days he was going to revisit this place, starting at this particular intersection, to examine every possible angle, every conceivable point of view?

The shadow of the lamppost grew longer. It prowled over to the pavement on the other side, where it lost its sharpness. The evening breeze turned overhead with a shriek, only to fall into a whoosh. Michael imagined it whispering, of all things, of murder at dusk. What a crazy idea! Where did that come from?

At 8:03pm came the sound of footfalls. A teenage girl was walking down the street so fast that the uneven click of her heels was already passing him by, leaving a faint whiff of perfume. No, that must have been some other fragrance, perhaps the saltiness of the sea, drifting over the sweetness of creek milkweeds and Belladonna lilies.

Where had he seen her before?

By the time he got out of the car, the girl had already crossed to the other side. With each step, the white dress whipped across her legs and fluttered, fold upon fold, in the cold wind.

His soles beat an echo in the empty street. He didn't mind the occasional squeak, because he had just bought them.

Electric lights buzzed in the buildings behind him, and foxtail ferns hissed, swaying along the trail. Her shadow flitted over the shrubs, falling farther and farther out of reach.

Before reaching the bend, she glanced over her shoulder and for a heartbeat, met his eyes. In some ways she reminded him of his ex-girlfriend, Ash, whom he hadn't seen since the *incident*. What was it that drew him to this girl? Why was he looking, time and again, to save a damsel in distress?

There was a certain quality about that look, which he couldn't put into words. Anguish? No, it was more acute than that. The closest he could name it was fear.

Excerpt: A Peek at Bathsheba

W rapped in a long, flowing fabric that creates countless folds around her curves, she loosens just the top of it and lets it slide off her head—only to reveal a blush, and mischievous glint, shining in her eye. It is over that sparkle that I catch a sudden reflection, coming from the back window, of a full moon.

Looking left, right, and down the staircase, to make sure no one is lurking outside my chamber door, I let her in. Then I lock it behind her, so no one may intrude upon us.

In a manner of greeting I raise my goblet. It is a gift from my supplier, Hiram king of Tyre, and unlike the other goblets I have in my possession, this one is made of fine glass, with minute air bubbles floating in it. With a big splash I fill it up to the rim with red, aromatic wine. In it I dip a glistening, ruddy cherry, and offer it to her, with a flowery toast.

"For you," I say. "With my everlasting love!"

Bathsheba takes the goblet from my hand, and raises it to her lips. "Love, everlasting?" she says, raising an eyebrow. "What does that mean, in this place?"

I hesitate to ask, "What place is that?"

"This court," she says, with a slight curtsy, "where the signature feature is a harem, which is as big as the king is endowed with glory."

"Glory is a good thing," say I, lowering my voice. "But sometimes it is better to meet in the shadows."

"Especially," she says, matching her voice to mine, "when there are so many others."

"Here we are," say I. "It's just us."

"Really," says Bathsheba, sipping her wine and ever so delightfully, licking her lips. "It must be a special night, then! Just you and me, and no one else, no one else at all."

Yet I cannot avoid feeling the presence of someone other than me in her thoughts, perhaps her husband, Uriah, who is one of my mighty soldiers and the most trusty of them. Earlier today he must have received his transfer orders to join the cavalry in the eastern hills, where he would be stationed outside the city of Rabbah.

I have a catch in my throat as I tell her, "I'm so glad you came."

Bathsheba lifts her eyes and looks straight at me.

"Really," she says, in her most velvety tone. "You mean, I had a choice in this matter?"

Her question stumps me at first, because how can I admit that she is right, so right in asking it? Instead I just shrug.

"You do have a choice," I say at last. "And I hope you'll make it."

"I'm so glad to hear that," says Bathsheba. "With that ape, I mean, that bodyguard of yours knocking so loudly, so rudely, and for such a long time at my door, I had my doubts about it."

"You can go, if you wish," I stress, with a reluctant tone. "But I wish you wouldn't. Stay with me, tonight."

Bathsheba picks the stem of the red cherry, and takes little bites out of it. In her pleasure she hums, and smacks her lips. Then she raises the goblet to my lips, letting me take in the aroma. I do, and then I take a long gulp.

With a slight sway of her hips Bathsheba walks past me, knowing I cannot take my eyes off of her. She wanders about my chamber as if she were the one owning it.

"You've been brought here by my order," I whisper to her, across the space. "But I am the one held captive."

Books by Uviart

Coma Confidential

(Volume I of *Ash Suspense Thrillers with a Dash of Romanc*e)

Kindle: B07L92YHST Paperback: 978-1791691592

Overkill

(Volume II of *Ash Suspense Thrillers with a Dash of Romance*)

Kindle: B084GDK156 Paperback: 979-8644328192

Overdose

(Volume III of *Ash Suspense Thrillers with a Dash of Romance*)

Kindle: B07VP4S6PK Paperback: 978-1086703665

Overdue

(Volume IV of *Ash Suspense Thrillers with a Dash of Romance*)

Kindle: B08S724T4G Paperback: 979-8599499671

Ash Suspense Thrillers: Trilogy

(Volume I-III of *Ash Suspense Thrillers with a Dash of Romance*)

Kindle: B0893MJNSY Paperback: 979-8648269644

Virtually Lace

(Volume I of *High-Tech Crime Solvers*)

Kindle: B07L968RXD Paperback: 978-1790407187

My Own Voice

(Volume I of *Still Life with Memories*)

Kindle: B013TA3FBS Paperback: 978-0984993215

The White Piano

(Volume II of *Still Life with Memories*)

Kindle: B013TAU7L4 Paperback: 978-1517049447

The Music of Us

(Volume III of *Still Life with Memories*)

Kindle: B013TCYWHC Paperback: 978-0-9849932-9-1

Dancing with Air

(Volume IV of *Still Life with Memories*)

Kindle: B01I4ENROY Paperback: 978-1536896534

Marriage before Death

(Volume V of *Still Life with Memories*)

Kindle: B0746NW5CD Paperback: 978-1974001736

Apart from Love

(*Still Life with Memories Bundle I*)

Kindle: B006WPITP0 Paperback: 978-0-9849932-0-8

Apart from War

(*Still Life with Memories Bundle II*)

Kindle: B07MMZLD7Z Paperback: 978-1792131592

Rise to Power

(Volume I of *The David Chronicles*)

Kindle: B00H6PMZ0U Paperback: 978-0-9849932-4-6

A Peek at Bathsheba

(Volume II of *The David Chronicles*)

Kindle: B00LEPPDV6 Paperback: 978-0-9849932-7-7

The Edge of Revolt

(Volume III of *The David Chronicles*)

Kindle: B00Q5WVKA6 Paperback: 978-0984993284

The David Chronicles: Trilogy

(Volume I-III of *The David Chronicles*)

Kindle: B00QYGF6WG Paperback: 978-1797440699

The David Chronicles: Art

(Volume IV-XI of *The David Chronicles*)

Kindle: B08YWSH7HC Paperback: 979-8721612886

Inspired by Art: Fighting Goliath

(Art book. Volume IV of *The David Chronicles*)

Kindle: B01MSBNSE4 Paperback 978-1797726212

Inspired by Art: Fall of a Giant

(Art book. Volume V of *The David Chronicles*)

Kindle: B01MSBS82Q Paperback: 978-1092307765

Inspired by Art: Rise to Power

(Art book. Volume VI of *The David Chronicles*)

Kindle: B01N2786VX Paperback: 978-1092263207

Inspired by Art: A Peek at Bathsheba

(Art book. Volume VII of *The David Chronicles*)

Kindle: B01MUFS9OA Paperback: 978-1092306225

Inspired by Art: The Edge of Revolt

(Art book. Volume VIII of *The David Chronicles*)

Kindle: B01N6ZG0W8 Paperback: 978-1091306158

Inspired by Art: The Last Concubine

(Art book. Volume IX of *The David Chronicles*)

Kindle: B01N2AXQP2 Paperback: 978-1092302715

A Favorite Son

Kindle: B00AUZ3LGU Paperback: 978-0-9849932-5-3

Twisted

Kindle: B00D7Q3IY4

Paperback: 978-0984993260 Nook: 2940151689588

Home

(Poetry)

Kindle: B00960TE3Y

Paperback: 978-09849932-3-9 Nook: 2940151729468

Can We Still Love

(Poetry)

Kindle: B0GV3G23V4 Paperback: B0GY8Q1Y9Z

Virtually Yummy: Recipes that Inspire
(Cookbook)

Kindle: B085BDNDM5 Nook: 2940163988655

Apple: id1501182051 Kobo: 9781393589853

בית

(Poetry in Hebrew)
Paperback: 978-1494920968

Apple: id1302908918 Kobo: 9781540199966

Jess and Wiggle

Kindle: B013D1W0SM Paperback: 978-1494920968

Now I Am Paper

Kindle: B00YQS4O72 Paperback: 978-1494919429

www.ingramcontent.com/pod-product-compliance
Lightning Source LLC
Chambersburg PA
CBHW022044170626
46808CB00003B/1359